Hawaiian Mythology

Gods and Spirits of Ancient Hawaii

Table of Contents

Introduction

From the fascinating tale of creation to animism to the reverence for a vast pantheon of deities, Hawaiian mythology represents a complex belief system and a pillar of Hawaiian culture. Despite their mysticism and being banned by the Christian missionaries until the 20th century, Hawaiian myths survived by oral narratives passed down through generations and are still thriving today. The songs and chants tell those curious how life on earth was created on Po from utter darkness, with the appearance of the spirit of Keawe.

Later, the spirit evolved into different divinities, humankind, and other living beings. Due to this, it is believed that all beings share a kindred spirit and can use this for spiritual communication. According to Hawaiian lore, the ancient spiritual force (mana) inhabits even sacred words and inanimate objects. To this day, Hawaiian natives honor their religion regarding everything from animals to the smallest mountain rocks as their relatives.

From this book, you'll learn about each god and goddess of the Hawaiian pantheon, including their role in people's lives and how they were honored by locals throughout the centuries. Apart from representing the starting point of evolution, the gods (called Akua in Hawaiian) are also responsible for bringing different natural phenomena to life. They are honored according to the one they rule over. The book introduces you to their children, Ku, Lono, Kanaloa, Kane, and many others, who have significant roles in people's lives. Like their parents, each Hawaiian god's child has a unique symbol, preferences, and correspondences in nature. Some even have more than one, depending on when and how they evolved from the primordial spirit.

Followers of the ancient Hawaiian religion have different ways of communicating with other deities and spirits, from reaching out to them to waiting for signs to contact a person. The ancient chieftains learned that spirits are volatile and have different ways of manifesting themselves. It made the chiefs equally crucial as part of the traditions as the deities and the spirits. Some tales affirm the chieftains were the descendants of the gods. In contemporary approaches, chiefs are often worshiped through similar acts and practices as higher beings.

This book guides you through the different practices and ways to revere each entity in the Hawaiian belief system. Whether you are a practitioner wanting to refresh your skills or delve into the culture, you can learn everything to enrich your practice. Read on if you are ready to embark on this journey.

Chapter 1:

Basics of Hawaiian Mythology

Hawaiian mythology is a fascinating topic few people know much about. While gods like Maui have been popularized by media such as Moana, and most visitors to the state learn a little about the goddess Pele, a larger breadth of mythology remains unaware.

This book helps you learn more about Hawaiian mythology, giving you better insight into the indigenous Hawaiians' beliefs and the gods and goddesses they worship.

However, before you can learn more about the deities, you should better understand the Hawaiian mythology basics and the Hawaiian people's creation story.

The Hawaiian Creation Myth

The ancient Hawaiians had no written language and, therefore, no way of writing down their stories, myths, and legends. Instead, these tales were passed down orally and the ancient Hawaiians' creation myth is contained in a chant known as the Kumulipo. This chant takes about 3 hours.

According to the Hawaiian creation myth, the world began with darkness. From the darkness came two beings – Kumulipo, the male essence of darkness, and Po'ele, the female darkness. They gave birth to the creatures that live in darkness.

These creatures, in turn, birthed Pouliuli and Powehiwehi, who birthed creatures that live mostly in darkness, and with each birth, brightened the light of the earth a little more.

The creatures they birthed gave birth to Po'el'ele and Pohaha, who birthed the creatures living in the light before the coming of the dawn – the near-dawn.

Finally, they gave birth to Po'hiolo and Po'ne'a'aku, who gave birth to the pig (in some versions, the dog) and the rat, ending the night.

From the dawn were born the first man, Ki'i, and the first woman, La'ila'i. Additionally, the first god, Kane, was born, as was the octopus, Kanaloa. La'ila'i gave birth to humanity through her relationship with Ki'i. Through her relationship with Kane, she gave birth to the gods.

Kane lives in Kane-huna-moku, a cloud between earth and heaven. Kane-huna-moku is off the coast of Kauai and is also the home to the water of life, which has many magical properties, including returning deceased humans sprinkled with the water back to life.

How the Hawaiian Islands Were Created

The Hawaiian creation myth tells about the creation of the world; it does not inform how the Hawaiian Islands, in particular, were created. The gods at the center of the story are Pele, the goddess of volcanoes and fire, and Namaka, the goddess of the sea.

The two goddesses are sisters and daughters of the goddess of fertility, Haumea, the sister of Kane.

According to the myth, the two sisters were enemies and constantly fighting. During one particularly vicious fight, Pele attacked Namaka with fire, giving rise to the island of Kauai.

As their fight continued, the other Hawaiian Islands sprang up until they reached and created Maui. There, Namaka believed she had beaten and killed Pele – but Pele proved her sister wrong, creating the Big d Hawaii Island and the Mauna Loa volcano. Finally, Namaka gave up, accepting she would never defeat her sister in battle.

However, Pele never gave up her anger, and Mauna Loa remains an active volcano. Today, she lives in the Halema'uma'u Crater at the top of Kilauea, another volcano on the Big Island.

The Ḥawaiian Afterlife

In Hawaiian myth, the soul was separated from the body after death. Black Rock, on Maui, was where the soul left the earth and "jumped" into the next world. For this reason, in Hawaiian, it is known as "ka-leine-a-ka-'uhane," the "leap of the soul."

What happens to a soul after death remains shrouded in mystery? In one version of the myth, the souls of those who lived a good life would go on to Kane-huna-moku and live with Kane. However, some souls could not move on to the next life; they still had responsibilities and obligations on earth preventing them from moving on.

Additionally, some did not live a good enough life to reach Kane-huna-moku. They led a neutral life, neither good nor evil, and would live what was essentially a heavenly version of life as a human. They would repeat the patterns from their life in the afterlife. However, they would not be touched by pain or happiness, unlike earthly life.

The evil and those who did not worship the gods went to a barren land without water - a land always in the twilight.

In another version of the myth, the good would go on to heaven, ruled by Wakea, the sky father. He was the grandson of La'ila'i, the first woman, and created the heavens by throwing a gourd into the sky.

In contrast, the evil would go on to Lua-o-Milu, the land of the dead ruled by Milu, the Hawaiian god of the dead. Besides being the ruler of the Hawaiian underworld, he is also tasked with the responsibility of finding and trapping wandering ghosts and returning them to Lua-o-Milu.

Prayer in Hawaiian Religion

In the Hawaiian religion, prayer was an essential part of life. It was performed before doing several key tasks, including building canoes and homes, and when giving the healing lomilomi massage. Prayer was employed before healing herbs were picked for medicines, during wars, and during the Makahiki (or harvest) season.

The gods who were prayed to differed depending on the purpose. For example, during wartime, they prayed to Ku (known as Akua), the god of war. During the Makahiki season, they prayed to Lono, the god of fertility.

Additionally, several different sacred traditions were meant to be followed as part of their religion and honoring the gods. For example, men and women would eat food made in different ovens, and they ate separately from each other. Furthermore, women were prohibited from eating some foods, like pig and coconut.

Also, a series of restrictions were known as kapu. Some kapu taboos included banning overfishing, preventing most people from looking at or approaching people of great power, like chiefs, and separating women from the community during menstruation. One of the possible punishments was death if the kapu was broken.

Hawaiian worship also involved sacrificing to the gods. For example, one offering to Kane includes kapa, a cloth made by Hawaiians using the bark fibers of certain native trees and shrubs. Today, gin is one of the most popular offerings to Pele by visitors to Halema"uma'u Crater.

Besides offerings of items, Hawaiians would also make animal and human sacrifices.

The Different Gods in Hawaiian Mythology

There are three different gods in Hawaiian mythology:

1. The four major gods

2. The thousands of lesser gods and goddesses

3. Guardian spirits

The four major gods were the chief gods of the Hawaiian pantheon. They were the gods the

Hawaiian people turned to most often. These gods were:

Kane

Kane and his brother, Kanaloa, were the first two gods. He was the gods' progenitor and the Hawaiian pantheon chief.

He was the god of light, procreation, and forests. In one version of the Hawaiian creation myth, he is not born alone with the first man and woman. Rather, he is the one who forms these beings out of red and white clay.

In another myth, he is the father of Pele, with his sister, the goddess of fertility, Haumea.

Besides the creation of humanity, Kane was also linked to the dawn and sky.

Kanaloa

In one creation myth version, Kanaloa was an octopus, the younger brother of Kane, and the first man and woman. He was the god of the squid, an important food source for the ancient Hawaiians.

Although he was the source of important food, Kanaloa was less important than the other three of the four major gods. For example, temples to Kanaloa were rare because the other three were arranged in a version of the Christian Trinity after the first missionaries reached the Hawaiian Islands, the Father, Son, and Holy Spirit - Kane, Ku, and Lono, leaving Kanaloa out of the Trinity.

However, while he became less important in Hawaiian religion, he was regarded as the creator god on other Polynesian islands.

Ku

Ku is the god of war. He is also known as Kūka'il-imoku ("Snatcher of Land"), a reference to his role as a war god. As wars between tribes in ancient Hawaii were common, Ku was looked to frequently as a harbinger of success in battle.

Besides being the god of war, Ku was also the god of the forests, rain, fishing, and husbandry. Additionally, he was the god of sorcery.

Beyond his role as the war god, Ku is best known for being the guardian god of King Kamehameha I, the first ruler of the unified Kingdom of Hawaii.

As part of his reverence of Ku, Kamehameha I had numerous statues of the god built in Kona in Hawaii.

Lono

Lono is the Hawaiian god of fertility, agriculture, and rainfall. He was also the god of music and peace. The harvest festival of Makahiki was dedicated to him.

Besides being an agriculture god, Lono was also a healer god, and it was to him that Hawaiian healers prayed for medical help. Temples to Lono were dedicated for medical purposes.

Beyond the four major gods, there were thousands of "minor" gods in the Hawaiian pantheon.

However, although these gods were not as important as the four main gods, it doesn't mean they were unimportant. Many were held in extremely high regard by the ancient Hawaiians and continue to be worshipped today.

Some other prominent gods in Hawaiian mythology include:

Pele: Considered the creator of the Hawaiian Islands, the volcano and fire goddess is best known for her temper. Due to her temper, many of the prayers dedicated to her are aimed towards the hope of preventing further volcanic eruptions, which signal her anger. Visitors to Hawaii are advised not to pick up anything from the islands because taking them off the island will bring down Pele's curse of bad luck on the person.

Laka: The goddess of dance, the Hula is sacred to her, and the performance of the dance honors her. She is Pele's sister and also the goddess of the forest. She provides divine inspiration to people as they dance the Hula.

Hina: Other than Pele, Hina is perhaps the best-recognized goddess from Hawaiian mythology. She is the goddess of heaven and earth and Ku's wife (and sister). She is also the goddess of female fertility, making her an important deity in the mythology of reproduction.

Haumea: The Hawaiian fertility goddess, Haumea, is Pele's mother, among other children. She gave birth to several generations of humans using magic to transform herself into a young girl. She gave humanity the ability to reproduce via natural childbirth, stopping the practice of cutting open the mother (a dangerous procedure without modern medicine) as the only form of human giving birth. Her other children include the sea goddess Namaka and the shark god Kāmohoali'i.

Poli'ahu: A goddess of snow, Poli'ahu was an enemy of Pele. She lives at the top of Mauna Kea and prevents Pele from expanding her influence to the northern end of Hawaii's Big Island.

Kamapua'a: A god of wild boars, is the son of Hina and a mortal chief. He is best known for his love for and pursuing the goddess Pele. In some stories, the two are lovers or are married.

Kamohoali'i: A shark god lives in underwater caves between the Maui and Kaho'olawe Islands. Kamohoali'I was a benevolent deity who would go in search of sailors lost at sea. If the sailors fed him awa, a drink made of kava, he would help them return home. He is a brother of Pele and the son of Haumea.

Kuula: A sea god, Kuula controls the fish in the sea and is the god of fishermen. As the god of fishermen, he taught the people of Hawaii not to overfish and to share their catch with their communities to increase social bonds.

Maui: Although he is well-known due to his position in pop culture, he was not actually a god. Rather, he was a trickster figure and hero who was a human. Due to this, he is very rarely worshipped as a deity and generally not regarded as a god.

Finally, after the thousands of "minor" gods are the guardian spirits. These spirits, known as the ʻaumākua, are essential guardians of individual families and are sometimes considered the ancestors of those families.

The minor gods can take the forms of anything naturally occurring in nature, including animals and plants. They protect and judge the families they are connected to, guiding and warning them of dangers throughout their lives. As judges, they are tasked with punishing members of their families who break the law and commit crimes. Additionally, they are tasked as go-betweens between the gods and humans, acting as messengers of humanity's prayers to the gods.

Now that you know more about Hawaiian mythology, the next step is to learn more about the gods and goddesses. The next two chapters will look at some of the most important deities in Hawaiian mythology in greater detail and help you understand how they are worshipped.

Later, you'll learn about the children of the gods and goddesses and the spirits and chiefs. Keep reading.

Chapter 2:

Gods

Many gods and goddesses were in ancient Hawaii, where the locals worshiped these deities and lived among them. The people interacted with these forces of nature and observed their power around them. The religious practices developed for each god were specific to people's personal experiences with them. In Hawaiian mythology, a multitude of gods is referenced with great reverence. The "Akua," or gods, were a lot like regular folks in the sense they loved and fought, fished and hunted for food, and often fell prey to their desires. The only difference between the gods and humans was the Akua contained more power.

Today, each Hawaiian family tree stretches far back to the beginning of time and connects to one or multiple gods. The earliest ancestral Akua is Waikea, the sky god, although he's not as well-known and worshiped as other major deities. This chapter dives into the world of the ancient gods and how they came to be the way they are. Methods of worshiping and other details are also discussed, so keep reading to find out more.

Major Deities

The Hawaiians worship countless deities and Akua, with thousands of gods, each with specific responsibilities. Among these, the four main gods worshiped by many people include Kane, Kanalua, Lono, and Ku. Waikea is also considered a major god, but there aren't many stories and myths associated with this deity. Each deity manifest in a different form, and most communities are seen worshiping different embodiments of these Akua.

1.   Waikea

Waikea, or Wakea, the sky father, is considered the god of light and the ruler of the heavens. He's the eldest son of "The Ancient One" and married to Papahānaumoku or Papa, the earth mother. They are considered the parent couple to the rest of the gods and goddesses. The name Waikea means space, or heaven, which symbolizes the sky. The best time to worship to connect with the sky god would be in the mornings.

The origin story of Hawaii comprises Wakea using Calabash to make the world. He used the cover to make the sky. The pulp of the Calabash was turned into the sun, and the seeds became the stars. The Calabash's white lining was made into the moon, and the white meat became the clouds. Another story about Wakea is of his firstborn being stillborn without any arms or legs. So, Wakea buried him outside his hut. The next morning, a plant grew where they had buried his body, and he was reborn as Ha-loa, meaning "first stalk."

2. Kane

Kane is considered the most influential god of the four major gods. Known as the god of creation, he represents the chiefs of Hawaiian tribes. According to legend, Kane was the creator of the three worlds, the upper heaven, the lower heaven, and the earth, created for mankind. He furnished the earth with sea creatures, animals, birds, and plants. Therefore, he is considered the father of living creatures. Although Kane plays a dominant role as the creator, he is assisted by Lono and Ku. There are many versions of the legend of creation, one of which is:

"The three gods, Kane, Ku, and Lono, lived in continual darkness, or night, when they decided to create light. They create three heavens for each and a resting place called the great earth of Kane. He created the sun, moon, and stars and placed them in a space between the earth and heaven. The first human was created using clay from all four corners of the earth. Kane and Ku breathed into the nostrils of the man, and Lono breathed into the mouth to give him life. He was named Honua-ula and was given a beautiful garden to live in. His wife was shaped from his side, named Lalo-hana."

Kane was worshiped unlike other gods and did not require human sacrifices or laborious rituals. Kane worshippers were distinguished from others and considered a consecrated class. A single conical stone was used to set up a family altar for worshiping Kane. At the altar, family members prayed to seek forgiveness and ask for protection with prayers and offerings. The stone was sprinkled with water or coconut oil during the ceremony and covered with bark.

For temple worship, a scaffolding was erected containing three stages, each representing the three worlds, earth, heaven, and upper heaven. Different prayers were offered on each step of the scaffolding, including the enumeration of Kane's names. Since Kane represents the creation of new generations, when people had trouble giving birth, they would present offerings to Kane and ask for his help. They would also say prayers when building something and needed Kane's blessings.

3.   Kanalua

Kanalua or Kanaloa is the opposite of Kane. Where Kane is all skies, creation, and dawn, Kanalua is associated with death and darkness. Hawaiian legend directly associates Kanalua with Kane as his opposing force, and many stories depict their adventures together. Kanalua is the god of the sea and the underworld. He is connected with everything sea-related, like sailing, fishing, or swimming. His symbols usually have depictions of squid or octopus. There are many myths about Kanalua's strife against Kane; one played out as described below:

"After the first company of spirits were sent down from heaven to the earth, Kanalua led them to rebel against Kane and the rest of the gods because they were not allowed to drink awa. However, they failed to win their battle and were cast down to the underworld where Kanalua became their ruler."

Other stories also depict Kanalua as the evil counterpart of Kane. One legend places Kane and Kanalua at opposite ends. When Kane created the first human, Kanalua also created one. However, Kane's human lived, but Kanalua's human remained a statue. As a result, Kanalua got angry and cursed humans to die. The worship of the god Kanalua was similar to Kane. Temple worship was the most prevalent for this deity.

4.   Lono

Associated with agriculture, fertility, rainfall, and music, the god Lono is one of the four major deities present before the creation. Many people also considered him the messenger god because of his association with clouds and storms. Unlike Kanalua, Lono was a god of peace and tranquility, with many legends depicting him coming to Earth on a rainbow. Prayers to Lono usually connect him to rainbows, clouds, storms, thunder, wind, and earthquakes.

A myth surrounding Lono is the legend of Makahiki, where Lono sends two of his brothers to earth to find him a wife. They travel to the ends of the earth and finally find the beautiful and kind Laka in Waipio valley. Lono descends to Earth on a rainbow and marries Laka. They live together and delight in many sports, especially surfing. However, a chief of earth woes Laka, and when Lono hears of this, he gets extremely mad and beats her to death. Right before she dies, Laka convinces Lono of her innocence, and Lono initiates the Makahiki games in her honor.

Lono worshippers set up prayers and offerings to pray for abundant crops, rain, and healing. For the god of fertility, the Makahiki festival was celebrated during the rainy season, which lasted four months. During this festival, people would leave their day-to-day occupations to participate in athletic competitions, as Lono was also associated with sports. A ten to fifteen feet long straight wooden post would depict this deity during these festivals. At the upper end of this post, a bird-like figure was etched. Feather wreaths and white streamers were hung along this post.

Each district contributed offerings to the god Lono. The statue was brought to the side of the sea-coast, and the procession would move from there. At each chief's place, the statue's carriers were fed, and a white streamer would be tied to the god. The chiefs would attach an ivory tooth to the statue, and prayers would be said. Signs of Lono's approval included the clouds gathered above the festival.

5.   Ku

Ku is considered the god of war, strength, and healing. Ku translates to rising upright and refers to the sun when it's rising. Ku is the husband of Hina, the moon goddess, and together they make up the ancestral gods of heaven and earth. The east direction is preferred when praying to Ku, while the opposite is true for Hina. Ku and Hina represent mankind's generations, those who are to come into this world and those already born.

Ku is worshiped for better crops, fruitful fishing, prosperity, and long life. He is also called upon to help heal from sickness and to get out of trouble. Ku is also represented by breadfruit, coconuts, hawks, and the ki leaf. Ku was the only god who required human sacrifice, so people presented their sacrifices on his altar, but soon enough, this ritual was taken out of practice.

Lesser Gods

Apart from the four major gods and the sky god, there were numerous lesser gods that people worshiped and still do. These subordinate gods came from the line of one of the major gods, and each had a purpose or responsibility. Each person would worship the gods that presided over the aspect of life they needed help with. Detailed below are some of the thousands of gods mentioned in Hawaiian mythology.

1. Kahoali

The dark god of sorcerers, Kahoali, was greatly feared because of his curses. Legend says he loved his drink with the human victim's eye. Therefore, human sacrifice was also his thing. He was said to make coral, or wooden figures, which he would bring to life to do his bidding. Kahoali was married to Paluhu, the goddess of sorcery. His worshippers were held in high regard, and especially his priest was respected and feared. The nemesis of Kahoali was Lono because he had the power to cure any curses or diseases inflicted by Kahoali.

2.   Kamohoali'i

The chief of many Hawaiian shark deities, Kamohoalii, or Kamoho, was the shark god. He was Pele's brother, the fire goddess, and considered the guardian of the island. Kamoho was also the ruler of the were-sharks or shark men. These were greedy humans who Kamoho cursed to turn into sharks periodically. They were recognized by shark tattoos on their backs, given by Kamoho.

3.   Puenui

The Hawaiian god of owls, Puenui, had the power to restore life to the wandering spirits he would encounter on his nocturnal hunting journeys. He was the lord of all the night-flying birds and loved to feed on the dwarves and elves of the Hawaiian Islands. Since he was associated with the night, he fell in love with the moon goddess, Hina. However, she rejected his love, so the nightly coo-ing of owls is a reflection of his sadness and mournful longing.

4. Pakaa

Pakaa, the Hawaiian god of wind, played a crucial part in one of the major wars between the deities. Pakaa is also credited with the invention of the sail to help humans travel faster by sea. In another myth, Pakaa assisted the hero Moikeha in winning a sailing race and won the hand of the daughter of Puna, the king of a Hawaiian Island.

5. Kaulu

Kaulu is a trickster god who's not only strong in physical strength but is also very powerful with magic. He has countless tricks up his sleeves and deceives gods and humans throughout the stories in Hawaiian mythology. He can be violent and destructive at times. Another one of his powers is shapeshifting into animals and even inanimate objects, which makes it much easier for him to trick others.

6. Ku'ula

Ku'ula is the god of the fish of the sea. He is said to get his power from the major god Ku. Legend states that the god Ku possessed his body leading to miraculous mana, or power entering his body, which was retained even after Ku left the body. So, Ku'ula got the power to control and influence all marine life as he pleased.

7. Kamapua'a

Kamapua translates to hog-child, and he got this name due to the story behind his birth. The son of moon Goddess Hina and Kahikiula, the chief of Oahu, Kamapua, was born to a jealous and vengeful father. The moon Goddess Hina was involved with Kahikiula's younger brother, which made the chief extremely jealous. After the birth of his son, the chief refused to accept Kamapua as his son and named him hog-child. So, Kamapua's childhood was full of hateful scorn and mocking. When he was old enough, he left Oahu with plans of revenge, which he later successfully enacted. Kamapua had the power to control rain and storms. He was also the lover of the powerful fire Goddess Pele as opposites attract.

8. Ukupanipo

Another shark god, Ukupanipo, can control the amount of fish near a fisherman. Therefore, he is often worshiped by fishermen and people traveling by sea. Since he controls the sharks, he is worshiped to protect against shark attacks. According to Hawaiian myth, he occasionally adopts a human child, which allows him to transform into a shark. The kid is then marked with shark symbolism under their shoulder blades.

Gods and goddesses were highly revered and feared. They could cause havoc across vast regions and simultaneously create peace and tranquility.

There are countless other lesser gods and deities that couldn't make it to this chapter, but the ones worth mentioning are discussed. Hawaiian myth and lore had a strong origin. However, the stories got mixed up and confused due to the ever-changing generations. Yet, most of the fundamental concepts remain the same. The gods and goddesses took care of the Hawaiian Islands and still do. The ways and traditions of worship remain almost the same as in the early times. Festivals and rituals help pay tribute to the gods and invoke their blessings.

Chapter 3:

Goddesses

Although Hawaiian mythology is rich with supernatural deities, there's not much mention of the goddesses in literature. However, on a deeper level, the goddesses played a primary role in keeping the peace and performing their respective responsibilities just as their male counterparts. There were so many goddesses in Hawaiian myth it is not possible to mention all of them in this chapter. However, seven of the most important goddesses will be the main focus of this discussion. Other lesser goddesses are also discussed briefly.

Major Deities

Papa

According to legend, Papa was the earth mother, the goddess who married Wakea, the sky father. The word Papahānaumoku translates to a place that gives birth to islands. Known as Mother Earth, Papa is considered the ancestor of the Hawaiian people. She is the epitome of peace, abundance, thankfulness, fertility, and providence. Her symbols include rainwater, rocks, and harvested foods.

Many legends surround Papa. According to one legend, she wed the sky father, Wakea, and had a daughter with him named Ho'ohokukalani. However, as the girl aged, Wakea fell in love with her and desired an intimate relationship with her. He tricked Papa into keeping her away so he could seduce Ho'ohokukalani. Their firstborn child was stillborn and buried by Papa.

Papa is a central figure due to her loving and forgiving nature. She nurtures human life on earth even after they misuse and damage the earth. It proves her loving personality. Her worship is usually done by women, as she is the primordial representation of giving life and healing. Many women's temples are built with the name "Hale O Papa," where the worship of this generous deity takes place.

Haumea

The goddess of childbirth and fertility, Haumea, is one of the major goddesses in Hawaiian mythology.

She takes many forms with the help of a magic stick known as Makalei. According to Hawaiian legends, she was extremely adept in midwifery and helped humans realize the natural way to give birth. Before this, humans would cut open the mother's stomach during birth, which was dangerous and unnatural.

The goddess was ageless, never retaining the signs of aging as other deities would. Although she frequently grew old, she would transform into a younger version of herself. Many generations went by while she kept this ruse of returning to the humans to sleep with her descendants to keep the generation going. However, her identity was eventually discovered, causing her to become angry and leave humanity forever.

Other legends connect Haumea with Kanaloa, the god of war. She had many children with him, who later became significant in Hawaiian mythology, which will be discussed in the next chapter. Haumea's worship is one of the oldest practices in Hawaiian traditions.

Hina

Hina is the moon goddess and the wife of Ku, one of the major Hawaiian deities. Together, they kept the balance of day and night. Other themes attributed to this beautiful yet eerie goddess include moon cycles, communication, and mediation. The lady of the moon takes many forms, as does the moon. She presides over death when in the form of the dark moon. As the full moon, she embodies the warrior spirit that every woman has in her. As the waxing moon, she becomes the creator and caretaker of humans, and as the waning moon, she becomes the aging crone, full of insight to share.

Many people consider her the intermediary between the gods and humans, although she required some persuasion. Numerous legends surround the goddess Hina because of her popularity compared to other goddesses. Consequently, many of these legends contradict each other, but they all tell the story of the beautiful, wise warrior goddess and strong female divine archetype. The famous legend connecting the goddess Hina with the moon tells the story of how she managed to live on the moon. Hina and her maidens would weave the softest kapa cloth required for many household purposes. However, the burden of so much work made her weary. Her resolve to leave earth got even stronger because of her troublesome family, her unruly sons, and her lazy husband. So, she decided to leave earth through the pathway of her rainbows.

First, she decided to go to the sun. During her ascent along the rainbows, she climbed and kept climbing until the sun's scorching heat was no longer bearable. Even the clouds left her, leaving her tortured and shriveled from the sun. Drained of all her power, Hina slipped down the rainbow and back to earth. She rested one day until her powers returned and decided she would find a place on the moon. As she sought to begin her journey, her husband caught wind of what was happening and begged her not to go. However, Hina's mind was set, and she kept climbing higher and higher. Her husband jumped after her and grabbed her foot in a last-minute effort, but even this did not deter the goddess, and she continued her climb. When she tried to shake her husband off, he injured her foot. When she finally made it to the moon, she limped into her new home, where she rested forever.

Kapo

Kapo, the Hawaiian goddess of sorcery, magic, and fertility, is a fiery yet brave goddess who knew many forms of dark magic. The daughter of Haumea, and sister to the fire goddess Pele (Pele will be discussed in the next chapter with the other children of the gods), Kapo was a true force of nature. She was also very apt in herbal medicine and used it during countless battles.

The most famous legend involving Kapo is when she saved her sister Pele from being forcefully intimate with the mischievous pig god, Kamapua. According to the legend, Pele was roaming around the gardens of one of the Hawaiian Islands when she noticed the god, Kamapua, stalking her. He was in a lustful and crazed state and tried to force himself on her. Seeing her sister in trouble, Kapo couldn't bear what was happening and devised a scheme of her own.

She sent her kohe lele, or flying vagina, into the air and directly in front of Kamapua to distract him. He immediately forgot about Pele and followed Kapo's kohe lele. He chased it as far as Oahu Island, where Kapo created a giant crater to trap the crazed god. Her worship consists of chants and offerings made in the goddess's name.

Kiha

Kiha, or Kihawani, was a dragon goddess and a known rival of Haumea. The legend surrounding the two is one of the most famous myths in Hawaiian mythology. Commonly known as the legend of Puna and the dragon goddess, the story follows the goddesses Kihawani and Haumea, who both wanted to marry Puna, the chief of Oahu. However, Haumea married Puna when her time came while being unaware that Kiha wanted Puna. One day, Puna and his people were searching for a good place to surf. When they finally settled on a place, they saw a beautiful woman (Kiha) floating on the water's surface.

She told Puna she knew a far better place to surf and could take him there. Unable to resist the temptation, Puna was tricked into following Kiha out to sea, far away from his people. Kiha took Puna to Molokai, where they continued to live. Although Kiha took care of her beloved and showed him all the love she could, Puna felt like a prisoner who couldn't escape the cave. Puna loved the ocean and missed his old life so much that he begged Kiha to let him visit the ocean once. Madly in love, Kiha obliged and let him go.

On the shore, Puna ran into his brother-in-law, Hinole. Hinole told him about Kiha's real form and how she kept him trapped and deceived in the cave. He told Puna how he could escape Kiha's clutches. When Puna returned to the cave, he stayed quiet instead of announcing his presence as Kiha wanted, and he saw her true form as a dragon covered with scales. He got scared and breathed fast; he attracted Kiha's attention, who, upon seeing him look at her in her real form, got extremely angry and threatened to eat his eyes. As soon as her anger passed, she went back to her normal form. However, by then, Puna had decided to carry out the plan Hinole suggested.

One day, Puna pretended to be sick, so when Kiha inquired what was wrong, he told her he needed special water from Mauna Kea. He knew Kiha considered herself strong and independent, so he told her he couldn't ask her to carry out such a difficult task as a woman. As expected, she fell for the trap and left to get the water. Puna handed her a jar with a small hole in the bottom to ensure the goddess stayed away as long as possible. Once Kiha was far enough, Puna escaped the cave and returned to Hawaii. He reunited with Haumea, and Kiha was left alone, angry, and betrayed. She tried to capture him again but failed.

Poli'ahu

Poliahu is one of the four goddesses of snow and ice. Not only was she exquisitely beautiful, but also extremely powerful for a lesser goddess. She's attributed to snow, sharpness, and athletic nature. She was the most vicious rival of the fire goddess, Pele. According to legend, Poliahu was a competitive athlete and loved to take part in holua, or sledding, which made sense considering she was a snow goddess.

Surprisingly, Pele was also very enthusiastic about this sport. One day, Pele challenged Poliahu to a race. They climbed the top of the mountain to reach the holua track. No doubt both goddesses were extremely talented athletes. However, as the race became more intense, the ground became hotter. After a while, Poliahu realized this was the doing of her rival goddess's powers, but she did not let it slow her down.

As Poliahu inched ahead, Pele lost her temper and summoned her absolute power to aid her in the race. As a result, the snowy mountain had great fire and molten lava fountains. Nonetheless, Poliahu didn't give up and used her snow powers to freeze the molten lava following her. Finally, Poliahu succeeded in defeating the fire goddess, Pele, in the race-turned-battle.

Laka

Laka is the wife of the fertility god Lono and is mainly associated with fertility, forests, nature, and vegetation. She is also the goddess of Hula, the traditional dancing style of Hawaiians. As the goddess of Hula, Laka is not just attractive and gentle but also quite inspirational. It is to her that the dancers pray before starting their performance. As the goddess of the forest, her other responsibilities include keeping the forest thriving and healthy.

Many of the flowers and plants associated with Laka are used to make Leis or flower necklaces.

These are worn during Hula performances. After each dance, these flowers are separated, taken to the ocean, and released in the water to honor the goddess of Hula. Today, many people pay tribute to the goddess by participating in Hula performances and saying prayers during the dances and after.

Lesser Deities

Hi'iaka

Hi'iaka is the daughter of Kane and Haumea. Although she's mostly known in Hawaiian mythology as the famous volcano goddess Pele's sister, she is a powerful goddess in her own right. She is considered the patron goddess of Hawaii and the Hula tradition. She is also the goddess of sorcery, magic, nature, and healing. Not only was she a talented magician and sorceress, but she was also an expert in medicinal and healing magic. Therefore, she was adept at detecting and deflecting any magic tricks. Hi'iaka was Pele's most trusted sibling and would often carry out tasks given by the volcano goddess.

One famous legend involving Hi'iaka and Pele was when Pele asked her sister to fetch her lover

Lohi'au. Hi'iaka had one request from Pele; to take care of her grove Hope. However, when Hi'iaka didn't return on time, Pele threw a fit of rage and destroyed her sister's beloved grove. Upon returning, Hi'iaka was heartbroken over her favorite grove being destroyed and established her distance and independence from Pele. The story of Hi'iaka is discussed more in the next chapter.

Lilinoe

Lilinoe is another snow goddess and is the younger sister of Poliahu. Like her sister, she has a great rivalry with the fire goddess Pele. However, she rarely acts on her rivalry and keeps away from Pele to ensure no fights ensue. Lilinoe is the spirit of snowy mountains and extinguished fires. Her name translates to "fine mist," so she is considered the Hawaiian deity of fog and mist. Lilinoe mostly served as Poliahu's handmaiden and would comb her sister's hair daily to make it soft and silky.

Unlike other mythologies and legends, the Hawaiian gods and goddesses were not directly related. The goddesses had a fair share in creating numerous traditions and history of Hawaiian culture.

Whether it was Hina with her legendary courage or Kiha with her burning passion, each goddess played an essential role in shaping culture. While no deity can be classified as entirely evil or good, they all made their fair share of mistakes and paid heavy prices in return.

Goddesses were equally as powerful as the gods and feared by the people. They could turn the world upside down in turmoil and chaos and instantly return it to peace and calm. Some goddesses were so unpredictable according to their moods and desires.

Each legend and story can teach a lesson, and each goddess can be a source of power and strength for women, even today. Their legends will never die.

Chapter 4:

Children of the Gods

Like the major gods and goddesses, children of deities were integral to the Ancient Hawaiian pantheon. Many tales and legends of their lives, adventures, and powers were told.

Children of the gods were incredibly powerful deities and had to prove their worth. They became incredibly powerful and presided over important forces of nature. Many others were descendants of deities—sometimes, they were siblings to other gods and goddesses—but were not deities. Even they possessed remarkable abilities that made them as highly regarded as deities.

With the multitude of deities in Hawaiian mythology, there could be thousands upon thousands of children of the gods. In addition, several variations of stories and myths of old gods and their children often existed.

This chapter focuses on the offspring of the most prominent Hawaiian deities. We'll cover some of their legends and explain their significance to Hawaiian people. Several children of the gods were associated with significant cycles, which is also covered.

Children of Haumea: Patroness of Childbirth

Haumea gave birth to many important deities in Hawaiian mythology. Although there are several accounts of Haumea's cycle, she is mostly believed to be the sister of the great gods Kane and Kanaloa. Countless generations of deities, humans, and other creatures sprung from Haumea's womb. Her godly children will be our focus in this section.

How Haumea ended up being a patron goddess of the Hawaiian Islands is unclear. According to some legends, Haumea takes many forms, notable as a deity and human. She also taught humans how to give birth naturally—before that, people would cut the mother open to deliver the newborn.

Haumea possessed a mystical Makalei branch and underwent several cycles of rebirth and renewal, thanks to her power to transform into a young girl. With each cycle, she returned to her homeland to marry her descendants and give birth to new generations of children.

These are the most important of Haumea's children, who are arguably the first children of the gods in Hawaiian mythology.

Pele: Goddess of Volcanoes and Fire

The highly regarded Hawaiian goddess of fire is associated with many tales and legends. The name Pele corresponds to volcanoes and their flowing lava. Several different stories of Pele's birth spun across the Hawaiian Islands, but she was almost always considered the daughter of Haumea. There's a particular legend that places Pele as the daughter of the sky god, Wakea, and the infamous goddess of the earth, Papa, but then again, Papa is sometimes portrayed as the deified form of Haumea.

The Many Legends of the Pele Cycle

Hawaiian mythology is packed with legends involving Pele. Although there is no definitive Pele cycle, she was largely associated with volcanoes and was the ruler of the Kilauea volcano presiding over many other fire deities. She was widely known for her fiery nature and ravishing beauty.

Pele's stories are drastically different. According to some myths, Pele has a father and is Haumea's only naturally-born child; the others sprung from her various body parts. The identity of Pele's father varies from one legend to another; it could be Moemoe, Kanehoalani, Kuwahailo, or Wakea—all are prominent gods in Hawaiian mythology. Another story says that Pele emanated from Haumea's thighs.

Pele's Migration to Hawaii

How Pele came to Hawaii is also contested. According to a dominant legend, Pele was fond of traveling and often roamed the Hawaiian Islands. She carried her sister Ni'iaka, born in the form of an egg, under her armpit or in her bosom, and headed to Hawaii. Throughout her cycle, Pele has several encounters with prominent figures. In particular, her encounter with Lohi'au, chief of Kauai Island, was significant—we'll explore it later.

In another legend, Pele was the daughter of Haumea and Kanehoalani and lived on the mythical Kuaihelani Island. Similarly, she had to carry her sister Hi'iaka and leave her, although not of her own free will—she was chased away by her older sister Namaka. Despite a few similar elements, this Pele cycle is drastically different than the one previously mentioned. We'll explore the story of Namaka and Pele in more detail later.

Pele's Worship

Most variations of the Pele cycle speak of her genuine love for her little sister Hi'iaka. Pele ensured to protect Hi'iaka at all costs. Carrying her under her armpit or in her bosom is a great symbol of sisterly love. Since the two were inseparable, Pele and Hi'iaka were often worshipped together.

In addition, the Kilauea volcano is seen as sacred to Pele and manifests her immense destructive powers. As a result, offerings were made and rituals held in honor of the goddess Pele to seek her strength and protection, especially upon visiting her volcano. Worshippers also sought to soothe

Pele's hot-tempered nature through chants and song, which, in return, would calm the petitioner.

Pele's spirit is eternal to ancient Hawaiians. They believed Pele could be seen in many of her forms, including a gorgeous young woman, an old lady, or a small white dog. The color of her hair can be anything. Pele is one of the most revered goddesses in Hawaiian mythology, and worshippers are expected to pay their respects whenever she appears.

Hi'iaka: Goddess of Hula, Chants, Sorcery, and Medicine

The legend of Hi'iaka, daughter of Haumea and Kane, is packed with wondrous adventures. According to many legends, Pele's egg hatched into Hi'iaka. The name Hi'iaka translates as "carried egg." It is composed of "hi'I," meaning "egg," and "aka," meaning "embryo." In some legends, she was referred to by her full name Hi'iaka-i-ka-poli-o-Pele, meaning "Hi'iaka in the bosom of Pele."

Having traveled alongside her sister, Hi'iaka soon began journeying on her own across the Hawaiian isles like Molokai, Oahu, and Maui. She roamed the lands and encountered countless chiefs, spirits, demons, dragons, and supernatural entities. She had to defeat them using her wit and magic. Throughout her travels, she chanted to the rocks and created the infamous Hula dance.

The Legend of Hi'iaka, Pele, and Lohi'au

Hi'iaka's quest to find Lohiau is possibly her most illustrious legend. Back when Pele carried Hi'iaka across the Hawaiian Islands, they reached Kauai. Pele fell in love with the island's chief, Lohi'au, and set out to marry him in the most glorious ways. She continued traveling from one island to another, each time establishing a new home where she planned to receive Lohi'au.

Eventually, the sisters returned to their homeland, and Pele was eager to find her lover and bring him to Kilauea. Fetching Lohi'au meant crossing the many Hawaiian Islands and facing significant dangers along the way. No one had the courage to undergo this journey except for Hi'iaka.

Upon leaving Kilaueua, Hi'iaka had to climb the rough rocks of the volcano. Pele wasn't too happy about Hi'iaka's slow pace, so she granted her new powers and sent a guardian servant to watch over her. One power was the magic skirt, which would help her overcome many enemies throughout her journey.

The Battle of Pana'ewa

The Hawaiian Islands were filled with many hostile creatures. On her way to find Lohi'au, Hi'iaka's first major challenge was crossing the forest separating the Kilauea volcano and the ocean. Once she entered the large, dense woods, which turned out to be the domain of the mo'o—or dragon—Pana'ewa. The mo'o had two birds scout the forest and signaled any intrusion. Hi'iaka arrived and started chanting provocative verses aimed at Pana'ewa that were heard across the forest. As the birds brought in the news, Pana'ewa heard Hi'iaka's chants and instantly recognized her. A ferocious battle began.

Hi'iaka had to fight Pana'ewa and all the deities and spirits of the forest. Pana'ewa had the power to transform into an almost invulnerable fog body and launched successive attacks that Hi'iaka parried using her magic skirt. She also used a knife to cut down her enemies and her lightning skirt attacks to strike through Pana'ewa's fog, mist, and rain clouds.

Hi'iaka managed to slay all the forest gods but was deeply wounded and exhausted. She hid among her fallen foes while Pana'ewa kept looking for her. In the meantime, Pele heard the strong echoes coming from the forest and sent a powerful squad comprising Hi'iaka's friends and relatives. Pana'ewa's two birds finally found Hi'iaka lying in the forest, and she was ready to finish her. As Hi'iaka rose and prepared for a seemingly lost battle, Pele's reinforcements arrived and launched a thunderstorm, sweeping down Pana'ewa and all the gods of the forest into the ocean.

Hi'iaka's endurance and perseverance paid off in the end, partly due to Pele's assistance. As a result, the forest of Pana'ewa was cleared of all dangers.

Hi'iaka Meets Lohi'au

Hi'iaka continued her brave journey, defeating foes and making allies as she traveled. Eventually, she reached Kauai' only to find Lohi'au dead. Through prayers and chants, she revived him, hence the 'goddess of medicine.' She had 40 days to return to Pele before Lohi'au died again, but she didn't make it.

Pele grew angry and got the impression that Hi'iaka betrayed her and wanted to keep Lohi'au for herself. A ruthless, vengeful Pele wreaked havoc in Hi'iaka's sacred woods and killed Hi'iaka's close companion, Hopoe. Hi'iaka was appalled and retaliated by embracing Lohi'au for good. The two sisters fought, and Lohi'au died again and had to be revived by Hi'iaka. Pele was sorrowful about her deeds and allowed Lohi'au to choose. Who Lohi'au chose has been contested.

Hi'iaka's Worship

Hii'aka is the patroness of Hula and was paid tribute to through Hula dances, chants, and prayers. Hi'iaka is regarded as one of the most virtuous goddesses in Hawaiian mythology possessing unparalleled bravery, strength, intelligence, and loyalty.

Namaka: Goddess of the Ocean

Daughter of Haumea and the god of war and sorcery, Ku'waha'ilo, Namaka'o'kaha'I, meaning "the eyes of Kaha'I," is a powerful sea goddess, mostly appearing in the Pele cycle. Namaka and Pele are seen as sisters in creation. As patronesses of water and fire, their relationship led to the creation of the Hawaiian Islands.

The Legend of Namaka and Pele

Despite being sisters, Namaka and Pele had a very conflicting relationship from the beginning. The reason for their hostility toward one another is unclear. It was suggested that Pele married the sorcerer Aukelenuiaiku, Namaka's former husband, which upset the latter.

Regardless of the reason, Pele's quarrel with her incredibly powerful sister was the reason she had to migrate to Hawaii. However, Namaka continued chasing her from one island to another. She kept extinguishing Pele's fires and sending tidal waves that destroyed the homes and craters she dug. Despite being on the run, Pele struck back and kept launching craters that produced huge, dark clouds of smoke wherever Namaka landed. However, Namaka gained the upper hand each time.

Pele's brother, Kamohoali'i, the shark god, called for the family to help Pele. Namaka managed to fight them off all at once and defeat Pele. The latter retreated again, and the chasing away continued for a long time. Eventually, Pele gathered her strength and decided to take on her relentless sister single-handedly. It was a fierce battle, but Namaka emerged victorious at last; Pele was dead for good (or almost).

Pele's Spirit

Soon after tearing her sister's body apart, Namaka looked up and over the mountain of Mauna Loa. She saw huge clouds of red-glowing smoke that formed a lovely figure of Pele. It was Pele's spirit that Namaka would never be able to kill. Pele's sisters rejoiced at the sight and, led by Hi'iaka, chanted and danced the Hula.

Kamohoali'i: Shark God

Sharks and, naturally, shark gods were held in high regard by ancient Hawaiians. Kamohoali'i's name means "the shark-king." Indeed, he was the chief of all shark gods and is easily the most revered.

Kamohoali'i, like several other shark gods, could take many forms, including a human's. He established sea caves and several inland homes in many parts of the sea. He never settled in any one place but kept traveling across the ocean and the Hawaiian Islands. He possessed superb intelligence and navigational skills.

Kamohoali'i was known for his graciousness and benevolence. For instance, he would appear and guide lost ships to find their way. In return, sailors made offerings and promised not to harm sharks. According to some legends, sharks roaming the oceans around Hawaii were instructed by Kamohoali'i not to attack humans.

As previously mentioned, Kamohoali'i appears briefly in the Namaka-Pele cycle. He observed Namake's quest for vengeance and wanted to help Pele by gathering all her friends and relatives to defend her.

The Legend of Kamohoali'i and Kalei

Kamohoali'i's main story involves a young woman named Kalei. The shark god was fascinated by her beauty and kept coming back to the Waipio River to watch her from a distance. Kalei was a very talented swimmer and could dive flawlessly from the rocks above, which impressed Kamohali'i. The shark god wasn't confident in his ability to seduce

Kalei in his original form, so he turned himself into a handsome man.

One day, the weather was rough, and Kalei was being swept away into the unforgiving sea when the shark god quickly intervened and guided her to safety. The two became acquainted and eventually married.

This chapter covered the most notable descendants of major Hawaiian deities. We focused on Haumea's children since they possessed unique cycles and were central figures in Hawaiian mythology. Despite not being among the four major gods, their immense powers of creation shaped the world we live in. Their spirits still live and are worshipped across the Hawaiian Islands and other parts of the world to this day.

Chapter 5:

Spirits and Chiefs

Ancient Hawaiian legends evoke many important figures other than deities. Among these are spirits that appear in several cycles of gods and goddesses. There are many different spirits, each possessing specific roles, and capabilities. We'll start the chapter by covering Hawaii's most famous spirits and their importance in Hawaiian mythology.

The second part deals with another crucial Hawaiian group: the chiefs. After the deities, these are perhaps the most influential figures in Hawaiian mythology. The Hawaiian chiefs maintained their place in society throughout most of Hawaiian history. We explain where they originated and why they were central to Hawaiian mythology.

The Significance of Spirits and Chiefs of Ancient Hawaii

Spirits hold a significant place in Hawaiian beliefs. Like spirits from other religions and mythologies, Hawaiian spirits transcend the physical world and inhabit the sacred Hawaiian lands and seas.

Spirits, in Hawaiian mythology, are mostly posthumous manifestations of beings that once lived in the Hawaiian Islands. Spirits might have once been deities, demigods, humans, animals, or other supernatural creatures. They can take many forms and can inhabit even inanimate objects such as trees, rocks, and oceans, among other things.

In Hawaiian legends, spirits often watched over the lands and protected their inhabitants, particularly the deity spirits, usually worshipped by Hawaiians. Other spirits are associated with evil and destruction. While most spirits inhabit the underworld, or "po," many dd not get there and remain present as spirits in the physical world. They sometimes ruled over areas and controlled aspects of nature.

On the other hand, the chiefs were powerful humans that ruled over the Hawaiian Islands. They descended from deities. Naturally, the "chief" title was inherited. Each island was ruled by a high chief, called 'ali'i nui," with the help of subordinate chiefs. Due to their lineage, chiefs possessed divine powers and were sometimes worshipped as deities.

Hawaiian Spirits

Ancient Hawaiians believed spirits could appear in any form and shape. They controlled elements of nature and affected people's lives in many different ways. They appear on many occasions in Hawaiian myths and legends. Here are the most notable Hawaiian spirits.

Ancestral Spirits

The "aumakua," meaning "ancestor gods," is easily the most important spirits in Hawaiian mythology because they can be a part of everyone's lives. They were the deified form of deceased ancestors, continuing to exist as ancestral spirits. They are considered family gods who offer guidance and protection, grant favors, provide gifts, and watch over their family in return for reverence and offerings. Families worship their ancestral spirit in many ways, including chants, prayers, offerings, and Hula dances. In times of need, they can ask their aumakua for help and advice.

The aumakua lead the transition of the dead to the afterlife. Families were expected to show great respect to their spirits to be granted a safe passage after death. Aumakua can inflict bad luck on those who offend and disrespect them. Those who led a wrongful life were punished and abandoned by ancestral spirits, causing them to carry on as malevolent spirits where they died. They could continue to haunt their families for generations unless sacrifices and offerings were made.

Mo'o Spirits

The word "mo'o" translates as "lizard." In their original form, mo'os are reptile-like creatures of varying sizes; they can be tiny lizards or gigantic dragons. The Hawaiian Islands were packed with mo'os, or lizard spirits. They often guarded rainforests, rivers, fishponds, pools, and sea caves. These dangerous amphibious creatures could transform into several bodies and possess several magical powers. Several mo'o spirits appeared in Hawaiian legends.

Pana'ewa

From the previous chapter, you will recall the infamous mo'o Pana'ewa, who was encountered by the goddess Hi'iaka on her journey to find Pele's lover. Pana'ewa is a gigantic dragon-like mo'o who guarded a large forest near Hilo. The deadly spirit ruled the forest with an army of evil gods and spirits. He robbed or killed whoever dared to cross the forest, although he allowed some people to pass. Pana'ewa had two birds that scouted the area for intruders. His demise was in the hands of Hi'iaka, largely thanks to the reinforcements of her sister Pele.

Kikipua

Hi'iaka's path across the Hawaiian Islands was a long one. Not long after she defeated Pana'ewa, she encountered a female companion named Wahine'o'maw'. The two reached the cliffs of Moloka'i and found a bridge. As Wahine started to cross, Hi'iaka recognized that the bridge was, in reality, the tongue of a huge creature.

The creature was Kikipua, a female man-eating spirit who tricked travelers by disguising herself. Hi'iaka leaped into the air and attacked the mo'o with her lightning magic skirt. Hi'iaka chased her to her lair before finishing her off.

Mokoli'i

Mokoli'i, meaning "little lizard," was actually a giant lizard spirit and another mo'o slain by Hi'iaka on her journey. The mo'o guarded a sacred place nearby Kualoa, and sailors were expected to show respect by lowering their sails to avoid being crushed by the mo'o spirit. When Hi'iaka approached, Mokoli'i attacked her but never stood a chance. A ruthless Hi'iaka cut his tail, threw it far into the sea, and slayed him. Hi'iaka's encounter with the lizard spirit led to the creation of Mokoli'i Island. The mo'o's tail formed the island while the rest of his body became what is known today as the Ko'olau Mountain Range in Oahu.

Kanekua'ana

Not all lizard spirits were malicious or had to be slain by Hi'iaka. Kanekua'ana was a highly revered water spirit in Hawaiian mythology. She came from Kahiki, which meant any faraway island, and brought pearl oysters, fish, and plenty of seafood. Because of her, the area where she settled was called Ewa and later "Wai momi," meaning "water of pearl," now known as Pearl Harbor.

The water spirit was worshipped as a goddess by anyone who passed by. She was called upon whenever food was scarce. For ages, Kanekua'ana brought her blessings to the people of Ewa.

Night Marchers

The "huaka'i po," meaning "spirit ranks," is a famous group of death-dealing spirits in Hawaiian mythology. These night marchers appear as ghost warriors and have escorted high chiefs on their way to battle in their previous life. The warrior spirits will eternally march through the forests and cities of Hawaii and can appear at any time of the night.

Common people who stumbled across the huaka'i po knew not to glance at them; the slightest eye contact could mean death. They expect everyone to avert their eyes, look down, and not speak a word. If interrupted, the night marchers would yell "o-ia!" before killing whoever stood in their way. The only way for someone to be spared is if their lineage traces back to one of the warriors. The deadly ghosts carry torches visible from afar and beat their drums for people to hear to warn commoners.

While the night marchers typically have specific paths to take, they can occasionally change their route for several reasons. They can also be invoked, even inadvertently. It is highly advised not to whistle at night as that can summon them. If faced with misfortune, witnesses are encouraged to lie low, play dead, and wait for the night marchers to pass. However, if shown respect, there is no reason for them to spill blood.

Man-Eating Spirits of Ni'ihau

Also known as the flying spirits of Ni'ihau, these fierce creatures guarded Ni'ihau Island. The legend tells the story of five fishermen named Ekahi, Elima, Eha, Ekolu, and Elua, who came from Kauai in search of food for their village. They knew the risk that awaited them, but they had no choice, as their village would starve to death.

A day passed, and the fishermen slept. The next morning, they woke up to find that Elima had disappeared. They feared that the spirit had caught him, but their leader reassured them that Elima had probably gone fishing. They woke up the next day, and Eha was missing. The next night, the three survivors slept close to each other and kept weapons beside them. However, that didn't stop the flying spirit from catching Ekolu and devouring him before his friends could do anything.

Ekahi came up with a brilliant plan to lure the creature at nightfall. They built a small house and set up two wooden decoys that looked like humans. This time, two man-eating spirits came and fell for the trick. Elua and Ekahi vanquished them with fire torches and returned home with plenty of fish and a tragic yet heroic tale to tell.

Milu, the Spirit of the Underworld

Milu is a divine spirit that rules over the underworld known as lua'o'milu, meaning the "pit or grave of Milu." Before he conquered and ceased control of the underworld, he was the chief of the Waipi'o Valley on the Big Island of Hawaii. The place is believed to hold the hidden entrance to the underworld.

Soon after he discovered the gateway, Milu established himself as the god of the dead and king of the ghosts. He commanded a myriad of spirits that would hunt escaped ghosts and bring them back to the underworld. Milu enjoyed the company of his "catcher spirits." Several tales mentioned how he kept the spirits entertained by teaching games and feasting with them.

Hawaiian Chiefs

The chiefs' lineage is traced back to Wakea, the god of the skies and heavens, and Papa, the goddess of the Earth. Hawaii had long been subjected to a caste system, and the ruling chiefs known as "ali'i" were the noble royalty. Since they were supposedly descendants of deities, the chiefs claimed divine power and ruled over the Hawaiian Islands. The symbol of the chiefs is the Kahili, a pole decorated with feathers at one end.

At first, the ancient chiefs didn't rule over lands. Only a few humans inhabited the Earth, and each family cared for itself. A few centuries later, the population grew, and the chiefs took over the land, establishing laws known as "kapu." It was a strictly enforced code of conduct that all commoners had to follow.

However, the chief's influence was restricted by another influential group called "kahuna," or priests. They descended from Wakea's brother Li-hau'ula. Kahuna were not only religious figures; they could be skilled or knowledgeable in any field, including medicine, craft, sorcery, navigation, and more. As a result, they were highly regarded in society. The highest-ranking chiefs eventually merged with the priests and established a new class of chiefs.

From there, chiefs were divided into many ranks and ruled over the Hawaiian Islands.

Ali'i nui

Among the Hawaiian nobility, the ali'i nui held the highest chief rank. During the time of Wakea, the title wasn't established. Only when all major Hawaiian Islands, notably Hawaii, O'ahu, Kaua'i, and Maui, were inhabited that the high chiefs start their actual reign over the people. Each ali'i nui ruled over an island and appointed subordinate chiefs to govern the island's districts.

The ali'i nui divided the land as they saw fit and possessed the right to discharge the lesser chiefs if they broke the codes of ethics. They were also responsible for establishing the 'kapu' code of laws.

Due to their lineage, ali'i nui were often seen as gods. So, people created chants in honor of their ruling chiefs.

The lineage of Hawaiian chief's traces back to some notable ancient ali'i nui, such as:

- Kumuhonua, ali'i nui of Oahu, son of the famous black magic wizard Maweke. Both were mentioned in chants. Kumuhonua was a descendant of Nana'ula, the first man from Kahiki to discover the Hawaiian Islands.

- Mo'ikeha, ali'i nui of Kaua'i, a brother of Kumuhonua. His heroic journey from Kahiki to Hawaii was celebrated in chants.

- Paumakua, the first ali'i nui of Maui. Paumaukua initiated a long line of Maui rulers and is mentioned in chants with several other Maui rulers.

Ali'i ai moku

The second most important rank of a chief is the ali'i ai moku. Each ali'i ai moku ruled over a district within an island. Since they typically had a similar lineage to the ali'i nui, they were highly respected, even by their superiors. They were often sovereign rulers of their districts.

Ali'i pi'o

Highly ranked chiefs were often careful not to break their rank. Chiefs can lose rank, for instance, if they marry someone with little or no rank. Sometimes they would marry their siblings to prevent losing rank. Their children would be called ali'i pi'o. These are no ali'i nui, but they are very highly regarded, sometimes revered as deities. Ali'i pi'o only spoke with people in the night-time, as restricted by their kapu.

Lesser Chiefs

There are many other different ranks of chiefs, based on what specific kapus they obeyed—these are codes of conduct related to taboos. Some ranks, especially the highest ones, were continually used to distinguish the noblest of chiefs, while others changed over time. The ranks are mostly inherited but can increase or decrease based on marriage. Low-rank chiefs were usually in service of the high chiefs.

Spirits and chiefs were an integral part of Hawaiian mythology. It is interesting and intriguing learning the importance of their existence in the history and culture of Hawaii and will remain for many generations.

Conclusion

According to Hawaiian mythology, the gods emerged from the deep darkness that ruled the universe. After the primordial spirit came to be, it slowly gave life to others, beginning with the first female goddess. At first, most Hawaiian deities had multiple roles. However, as their number increased, they took over different dominions. Nowadays, the followers differentiate between many gods. The deities of sorcery and guardian gods are worshiped due to the immense help they provide people. Hawaiians also honor their ancestors with the same regularity. According to the lore, ancestors that lived long before were the descendants of the gods, had divine powers, and many often became gods after death.

In Hawaiian mythology, each god, goddess, and their children and descendants have a unique name and traits. Their powers and acts are immortalized in the stories passed down through generations. They also have different associations, which helps followers honor them in a way that feels right to them. For example, Pele is known for her ability to raise fire and is celebrated with this element. Meanwhile, her sister, Namaka, is the goddess of the seas and is usually honored with water.

Sometimes the deities connect with people through different signs. Other times it's up to the follower to call on them. Either way, learning these signs is crucial if you want to connect to them and ask for their help or simply express your gratitude for the blessings they provide. Since people also have unique personality traits and preferences, everyone's experience when connecting to a Hawaiian deity will be different.

Spirits and chiefs are descendants of the gods and, therefore, have divine powers. It allows them to communicate with the divine like in ancient times. However, the two groups also have different roles in people's lives - inherently meaning communicating with them will also be a slightly different experience. As the closest offspring of the gods, the chiefs are considered nobility, although there are several ranks among them, which should be considered when calling on them.

Last but not least, the Hawaiian ancestral spirits are typically the guardian of the family they once were a part of. Due to their close blood relationship with the person contacting them, the ancestral spirits are the best source of wisdom in many aspects of life. It doesn't take much time to connect with them, so they're usually the first choice for many, including those reconnecting with their roots.

References

Love, B. (2018, May 23). Hawaiian Mythology (An Intro to Hawaiian Gods, Goddesses & Legends). Green Global Travel. https://greenglobaltravel. com/hawaiian-mythology-gods-goddesses-legends/

What Are the Major Elements of Hawaiian Mythology? (n.d.). Language Humanities. http:// www.languagehumanities.org/what-are-the-major-elements-of-hawaiian-mythology.htm

In The Beginning - Hawaiian Gods. (n.d.). Coffeetimes.Com. http://www.coffeetimes.com/ gods.htm

An Illustration Studio. (2013). Creation Stories. Createspace.

Brown, H. (2022, March 1). Hawaiian Gods and Goddesses – A list. Sea Paradise. https://www.

seaparadise.com/hawaiian-gods-and-goddesses-a-list

Derrick, J. C. (n.d.). Pele's Curse: Why you should never take lava rocks from Hawaii. Hawaii-guide.com; Hawaii-Guide. https://www.hawaii-guide.com/why-you-should-never-take-lava-rocks-from-hawaii

Grainger, A. (2022, January 17). Polynesian creation myths: Ever wondered how Hawai'i was created? TheCollector. https://www.thecollector.com/polynesian-creation-myths/

Hamblin, W., & Peterson, D. (2014, February 23). Diving into the afterlife in Hawaii. Deseret News (Salt Lake City, Utah: 1964). https://www.deseret.com/2014/2/22/20535821/diving-into-the-afterlife-in-hawaii

Handy, E. S. C., & Beckwith, M. W. (1940). Hawaiian Mythology. American Sociological Review, 5(6), 984. https://doi.org/10.2307/2084549

Hattie, H. (n.d.). The creation of the Hawaiian Islands. Hilo Hattie. https://www.hilohattie.com/blogs/news/the-creation-of-the-hawaiian-islands

Hawaiian Mythology: Part one: The gods: I. coming of the gods. (n.d.). Sacred-texts.com. https://www.sacred-texts.com/pac/hm/hm03.htm

Hawaiian Mythology: Part one: The gods: IV. The Kane worship. (n.d.). Sacred-texts.com. https://www.sacred-texts.com/pac/hm/hm06.htm

Hawaiian Mythology: Part one: The gods: X. the soul after death. (n.d.). Sacred-texts.com. https://www.sacred-texts.com/pac/hm/hm12.htm

Kāne. (n.d.). Myths and Folklore Wiki. https://mythus.fandom.com/wiki/K%C4%81ne

Love, B. (2018, May 23). Hawaiian mythology (an intro to Hawaiian Gods, goddesses & Legends). Green Global Travel. https://greenglobaltravel.com/hawaiian-mythology-gods-goddesses-legends/

Shaka Guide. (n.d.). https://www.shakaguide.com/planyourtrip/oahu/hawaiian-creation-story

Shute, M. (2022, July 7). These 9 fascinating stories of Hawaiian mythology will leave you shaking your head in awe. OnlyInYourState; Only In Your

State. https://www.onlyinyourstate.com/hawaii/hi-mythology/

What are the major elements of Hawaiian mythology? (2022, September 21). Language Humanities. https://www.languagehumanities.org/what-are-the-major-elements-of-hawaiian-mythology.htm

(N.d.). Hawaii.edu. http://www2.hawaii.edu/~suehaseg/Maluae.htm

Brown, H. (2022, March 1). Hawaiian Gods and Goddesses – A list. Sea Paradise. https://www.seaparadise.com/hawaiian-gods-and-goddesses-a-list/